Oscar and the Super

Written by Ann Dragich

Illustrated by Willow D'Arcy

Oscar and the Super

This is a work of fiction. One character, based
on the author solely in appearance and job title,
is used completely fictitiously. Any other
resemblance to actual persons or events is entirely
coincidental.

Written by Ann Dragich
Illustrated by Willow D'Arcy

amdragich@gmail.com
IG: Ann_Dragich_author_page
willowdarcy.com

ISBN: 979-8-9917951-1-1

Preface

    This story takes place on land once inhabited by the Munsee Lenape, Wappinger, and Wiechquaesgeck peoples. It was conceived in response to a class assignment while I was enrolled in the History of Theatre & Dance I: Myth, Magic & Madness at UC Davis- and written for my professor with the intent of expressing an understanding of course concepts including Shamanism, ritual, mimesis, masks, performativity, and illocution. In a past life, I had been the superintendent of a building in Harlem, and another building in Washington Heights. I found a parallel between a Shaman's connection to the land for his people, and my own connection to housing elements like water, heat and security for my tenants.

    The idea that Shamanism deals with the state of mind that people don't fully understand the world around us resonated with me. My tenants surely didn't understand the functioning of plumbing, gas, and electricity, but had absolute faith that the answers were within me. Sometimes they were, but sometimes, no matter how many ritualistic toilet re-seatings I executed, the ceiling below would still explode with water.

A Saturday Afternoon

HOUSE CLEANING
LOST CAT
Meeting in 3A
8PM Wednesday
Community housing
Watch Group
Know your RIGHTS
Landlords are
CROOKS!

My Mary married a broker, so I have it on good authority that the city has to make him fix that gate! The code says "self-closing" hinges!

SLAM!

Sometimes Ma would ask Mrs. Simmons to watch me when she worked late.

SLAM!

SLAM!

SLAM!

SLAM!
CRASH!

SLAM!

Mr. Raj, I want to thank you for taking my code concerns seriously. Now there is a matter of a noise nuisance when the gate shuts and—

I'm sorry Mrs. Simmons, you can ask your neighbors to close the gate quietly, or file a noise complaint with the police. I've got another call now.
CLICK

Oscar, hold these rags and this twine. We are taking matters into our own hands.

I will be pursuing this further, but at least we'll get some peace tonight!

That Night

BANG!

The rest of the night was eerily quiet, and there was an uneasiness in the air that left me too unsettled to sleep.

The Next Morning

The rags seemed to have multiplied. There was no way that the two t-shirts and the kitchen towel I had tied to the gate post could have generated this much debris.

We looked around the yard and up and down the street but couldn't spot a soul.

There are always two sides of a gate, kid. If you aren't careful when you put it together, a gate can open to the wrong side.
Of course there are two sides to a gate...

I didn't cause this, but my presence certainly made it possible.

Unfortunately, I am no longer welcome where one must go to find the things needed to fix this. But fix it we must.

The eye on Mr. Jefferies's forehead fixed on my face. I couldn't blink or look away. I felt like layers of my skin were being peeled away, and what was left of me could be frozen and shattered by the slightest breeze.

When his eye released me, I was shivering.
Kid, you have the ability to see and do what others can't. You are of my kind.

SPIFF PEANUT BUTTER

This feather will protect you, and this jar will hold what's needed.

You will also need a map.

You will fill this jar with the sap of the Sigillaria tree and the fruit of the Jujube, which will be found in the same place.

Back in His Room

After laying out my tools on the bed, I emptied my backpack and placed it on the floor– ready to be filled.

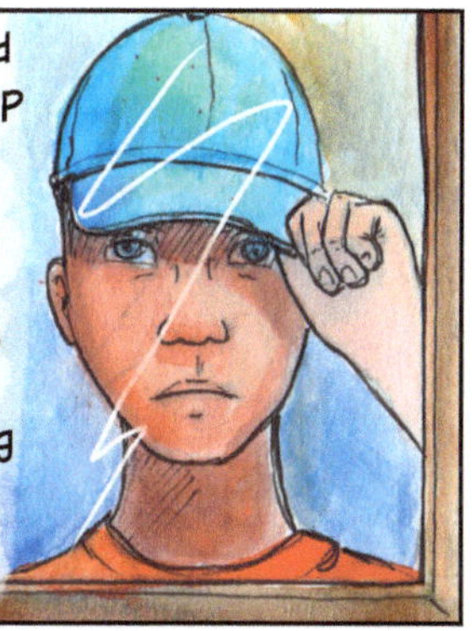

The day seemed to pass in slow motion. Everyone from the building seemed unsettled and displaced.

The men got drunk in the basement which prevented anyone from reaching the laundry machines.

The kids couldn't agree on a game to play and wandered the halls aimlessly.

The women sulked, and snapped, and produced wilted vegetables and stale coffee at dinner time.

7

Later That Day

As I approached the gate, Morning Star began to take shape and stepped towards me.

Follow me.

Come on now, don't lose your nerve before we've even started.

I took a few steps forward.

As we ran, I felt sensation returning to my limbs and blood beginning to pulse in my veins. The air was crisp on my skin and smelled of swamps, and ocean, and snow melting on pine needles all at the same time. I found myself enjoying the run. A feeling of freedom was permeating my being. My consciousness spread out, exploring the land around me. There was a lake to my left. I could feel the ripples the fish made as they swam. On my right there were tall trees, of the ancient kind. I could hear them whispering the secrets that only trees should know. Behind me was a slurry of dust and mist, pulsing and spiraling and erasing the trail of my existence.

My glazed eyes passed though the figure in front of me and she turned.

I felt something with weight hovering just out of reach.

After running for what seemed like several more minutes, but could have been any amount of time, we began to slow down.

Morning Star stopped in front of a giant hedge. It rose taller than most trees and expanded as far as I could see in either direction. The path we were following ran straight into a hole in the brush. Morning Star took my hand.

Reining my consciousness back in, I focused on narrowing my attention to my own body on the path. Something pricked against my skin. My hand went to my pocket, curling around a feather. Oscar! My name was Oscar.

The fox woman's warning was apt. My inhale whistled through my body like a speeding locomotive close enough to touch. My footsteps echoed like thunder. I raised my free hand up to test my vision. The blackness was so complete I wasn't positive my hand was still real until my fingertips brushed my forehead.

Morning Star tugged my arm. Adjusting my direction, I walked, taking special care in placing my feet even more gently with each step.

Her voice sounded distant and muffled, like it was coming from underwater. Right foot. Left foot.

Blinded by a sudden brightness, I stumbled uncontrollably.

I fumbled with the straps of my bag, then the zipper, and produced the jar and pocketknife. Morning Star swiftly took over, opening the knife.

The path home took forever yet passed in an instant. I clung to my name with the certain knowledge that if I let it go for even the slightest moment, this place would claim me, for now I was in possession of part of it.

I was home. The gate was vibrating behind me. Mr. Jefferies was standing in front of me, and Morning Star was back in her fox's body circling Mr. Jefferies's legs like a cat.

The Next Day

I woke, feeling sore and unrested. My mind was blank. I lay there for a few minutes, feeling my breath swirl in and out of my lungs. The memories rushed back in a jumble.

I leapt up, running to peer out at the front lot.

The End.

Mrs. Simmons

Building Style
TBD

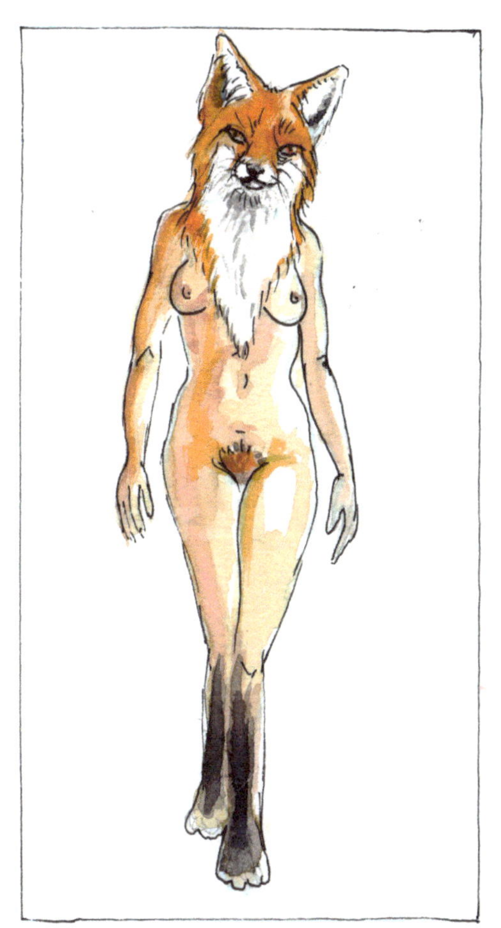

Thank you for reading.
Please look out for more short stories
from me in this graphic novel format.
I have another in the works as I write this.
I also plan to publish a book of my
tap dance notes (mostly in Kahnotation),
and a memoir about my time as a
building superintendent.